The Berenstain Bears®

We Love Our Dad!

We love our dad,
our ol' Papa Bear,
who does so much for us
and is always there!

Jan & Mike Berenstain

HARPER FESTIVAL
An Imprint of HarperCollinsPublishers

Copyright © 2013 by Berenstain Publishing, Inc.
All rights reserved. Printed in the United States of America. No part of this book may be used or reproduced in any manner whatsoever without written permission except in the case of brief quotations embodied in critical articles and reviews. For information address HarperCollins Publishers, 195 Broadway, New York, NY 10007.
www.harpercollinschildrens.com
Library of Congress catalog card number: 2012950646
ISBN 978-0-06-207551-2
15 16 17 CWM 10 9 8 7 6
❖
First Edition

Sister, Brother, and Honey Bear loved their Papa. They loved him very much. After all, he was always there for them.

He baited their hooks when they went fishing. He threw them fly balls when they played catch. He was their sled-puller on their way to the top of Dead Bear Hill.

BearCount
Hospital

He carried them on his
shoulders when they got tired
and rushed them to the doctor
when they were hurt.

He told them funny
stories and corny jokes.
He read to them at
bedtime, tucked them
in, and kissed them
good night.

Yes, the cubs certainly loved their Papa Bear. But sometimes they took him a bit for granted. After all, he *was* always there. They never even noticed some of the things he did—like working. Papa worked very hard. He worked in his shop all day making furniture. He worked fixing things up around the house.

He worked doing chores like mowing the lawn or shoveling snow or taking out the trash. It's true that Papa enjoyed working. But he enjoyed getting credit for it sometimes, too.

One warm spring morning, not long after Mother's Day, the cubs were talking about what they would do for Father's Day. Mama was listening to them nearby.

"Let's make Papa a big family album with pictures of us doing stuff with him," said Sister.

"We just gave Mama an album like that for Mother's Day," said Brother.

"Oh, yeah," said Sister. Honey Bear was looking out the window watching Papa mowing the lawn.

"Papa workin'," she said.

"What's that, Honey?" asked Mama.

"Papa workin'!" said Honey, pointing.

"Hmm!" said Mama. "Honey just had a good idea."

"She did?" said Brother and Sister.

"Yes," said Mama. "Your Papa works very hard. It would be a nice gift if you cubs did his jobs for him on Father's Day and let him relax."

Now that they thought about it, it was true—Papa *did* work all the time. He could use a rest.

"Way to go, Honey Bear!" said Sister and Brother, giving her high fives.

The cubs decided to make gift certificates that Papa could cash in for the jobs they would do.

All that day, they followed him around, spying on him. They checked off the jobs he did on a clipboard.

"Carrying wood," said Sister.

"Carrying wood. Check!" said Brother.

"Check!" said Honey.

"Painting the garage," said Sister.

"Painting the garage. Check!" said Brother.

"Check!" said Honey.

"Replacing loose tree bark on tree house," said
Sister.
"Replacing loose tree bark. Check!" said Brother.
"Check!" said Honey.

The cubs followed Papa the next day, too. They didn't put furniture making on their list because they didn't know how to make furniture.

But they did check off things like trimming the rose bushes, putting up fence rails, and cleaning out the basement.

That evening, they made a gift certificate for each job. The gift certificates looked like this:

Gift Certificate—Good for One Job
CLEAN THE WORKSHOP

Gift Certificate for One Job
CEMENT

Gift Certificate CLE A

Gift Certificate—Good for One Job
TAKE OUT TRASH

Gift Certificate—Good for One Job
WASH THE CAR

Gift Certific PLANT GRA

food for One Job
MOW THE LAW

The cubs couldn't wait for Father's Day to arrive so they could surprise him with their special gift!

On Father's Day, the cubs woke up bright and early. They waited until nearly six a.m. before running into Mama and Papa's room and jumping on the bed.

"Happy Father's Day, Papa!" they yelled.

"Huh? Wha?" said Papa, sleepily. "Is it Father's Day?"

"Of course it is!" said the cubs. "Open your present!" They gave him a big envelope. Papa thought it was a card.

"Why, thank you," he said. But when he opened it, the gift certificates spilled out.

"What's this?" he asked.

"They're gift certificates you cash in for us to do your jobs," explained Brother. "You can just relax all day."

"What a thoughtful gift," said Papa.

"It was Honey's idea," said Sister.

"Thank you, Honey!" said Papa, giving all his thoughtful cubs a big hug.

"I think I'd like to spend the day just watching football," said Papa. "It's Father's Day," said Mama. "You can do whatever you like." "Wow!" said Papa, settling down in his easy chair in front of the TV. "I could get used to this."

Papa cashed in his gift certificates and the cubs set to work. Their first job was washing the car. They got out buckets, soap, cloths, and the garden hose. They scrubbed and washed and rinsed. But the car still seemed a little dirty.

"Papa!" they called. "We're having trouble. Can you help us?"

"Of course," he said, looking things over. "You just need more elbow grease. I'll show you."

So Papa and the cubs scrubbed and washed and rinsed together. When they were done, the car was bright and clean and shiny.

"You go and relax now, Papa," said the cubs. "We'll do the rest." Their next job was cleaning up the wood chips in Papa's shop. The cubs got out dust pans, brooms, and a shop vacuum and set to work. They swept and cleaned and vacuumed. But the shop still looked a little dirty.

"Papa!" they called. "We're having trouble. Can you help us?"

"Of course," he said, looking things over. "You just need to give it more oomph! I'll show you."

So Papa and the cubs swept and cleaned and vacuumed together. When they were done, the shop was spic and span.

"You go and relax now, Papa," said the cubs. "We'll do the rest."
Their next job was spreading grass seed on the bare spots in the lawn. The cubs got out rakes and bags of seed. Brother raked the hard-packed earth while Sister and Honey spread the seed. But they soon got tired. There were still a lot of bare spots left.

"Papa!" they called. "We're having trouble. Can you help us?"

"Of course," he said, looking things over. "You just need more muscle power. I'll show you."

So Papa and the cubs raked and spread the seed. When they were done, every bare spot on the lawn was covered with new seed.

"You go and relax now, Papa," said the cubs. "We'll do the rest." But Papa shook his head.

"Actually," he said, "I'm getting bored just watching TV. It's more fun doing things with you. What shall we do next?

"How about a game of baseball?" said Brother.

"Perfect!" said Papa.

So the whole family played ball. Brother, Sister, and Honey took turns pitching, batting, and fielding. Papa was catcher and Mama was the ump. A wonderful Father's Day was had by all!

At bedtime, the cubs took turns jumping off their beds onto a big cushion.

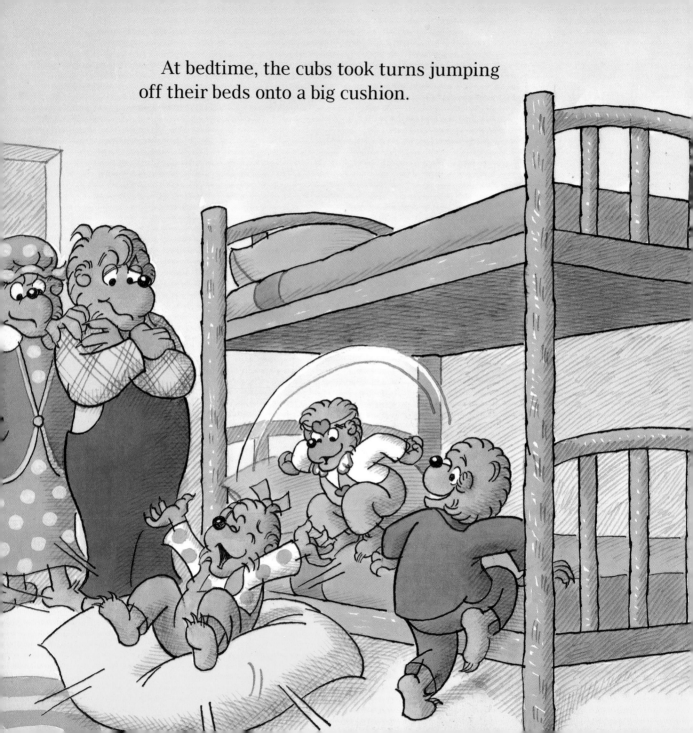

"It isn't fair!" said Brother as Papa helped him into his pajamas. "There's a Mother's Day and a Father's Day— why isn't there a Cubs' Day?"

Papa smiled at Mama Bear.

"I haven't the faintest idea," he said.

Papa and Mama tucked the cubs in and turned out the light.

"Did you have a good Father's Day, Papa?" asked Sister.

"Yes, sweetie," said Papa, kissing her, Brother, and Honey good night. "The best Father's Day ever!"